for
Elizabeth

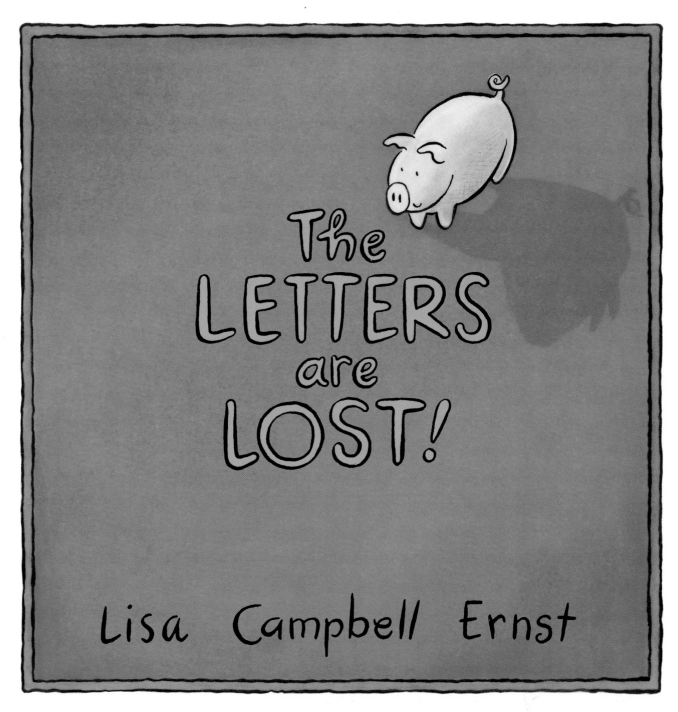

The LETTERS are LOST!

Lisa Campbell Ernst

 Viking

Long ago the letters were all together, neat and tidy.

But time passed. First one block disappeared, then the next, and the next, until now — their box is empty.

The letters are lost! Come, let's find them, one by one.

flew high in an Airplane.

tumbled into the Bath.

C joined a family of Cows.

D was a Dog's tasty toy.

found a home
with some Eggs.

took a swim
   with the Fish.

G stopped to look
through some Glasses.

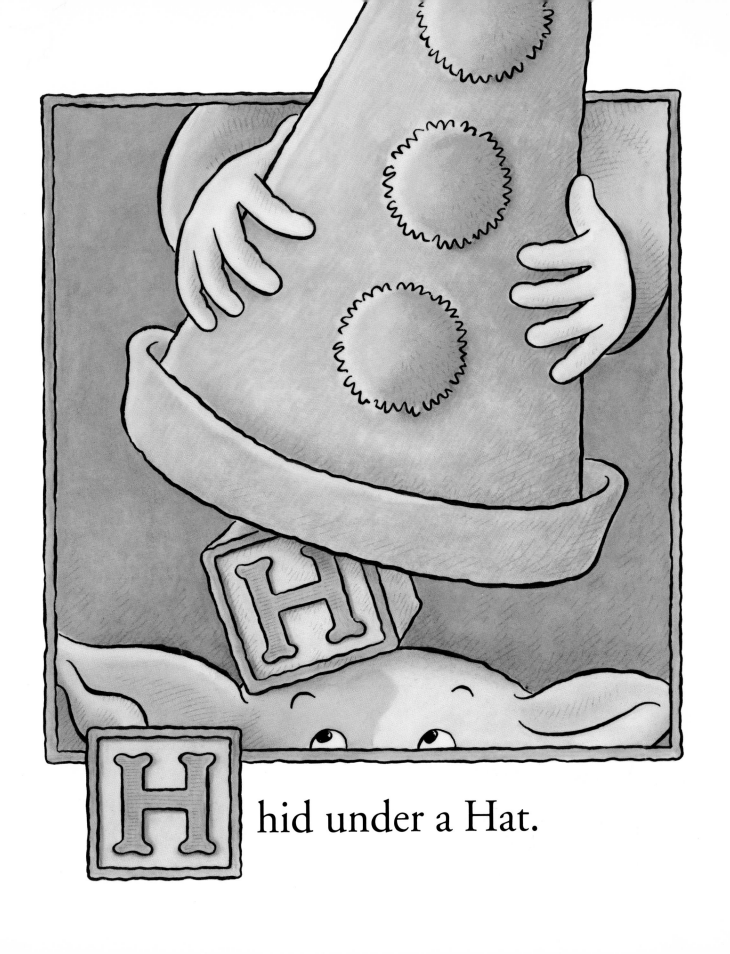

hid under a Hat.

I longed for strawberry
Ice cream.

J jumped out of a Jack-in-the-box.

hitched a ride in a
Kangaroo pouch.

landed in a pile of Leaves.

M admired himself
in a Mirror.

found a tower
of Numbers.

peeked through an Oval.

dove into the Popcorn.

took a nap on a Quilt.

R rolled away on
a Roller skate.

went to play
in the Sandbox.

helped to squish out
the Toothpaste.

turned herself
Upside down.

made a fancy Valentine.

W fell into the Washing machine.

played the XYlophone.

Z did a jig with a Zebra.

At last
the letters are together
again. But not
for long!

Soon the blocks will begin to disappear once more. Can you guess where they might go?

VIKING
Published by the Penguin Group
Penguin Books USA Inc., 375 Hudson Street, New York, New York 10014, U.S.A.
Penguin Books Ltd, 27 Wrights Lane, London W8 5TZ, England
Penguin Books Australia Ltd, Ringwood, Victoria, Australia
Penguin Books Canada Ltd, 10 Alcorn Avenue, Toronto, Ontario, Canada M4V 3B2
Penguin Books (N.Z.) Ltd, 182–190 Wairau Road, Auckland 10, New Zealand

Penguin Books Ltd, Registered Offices: Harmondsworth, Middlesex, England

First published in 1996 by Viking, a division of Penguin Books USA Inc.

3 5 7 9 10 8 6 4 2

Copyright © Lisa Campbell Ernst, 1996
All rights reserved

CIP data is available upon request from the Library of Congress.

ISBN 0-670-86336-X

Manufactured in China
Set in Garamond